T0199005

TOMMY
Takes Back His
POWER

To order additional copies of this book, contact:
Xlibris
1-888-795-4274
www.Xlibris.com
Orders@Xlibris.com

ISBN: Softcover   978-1-9845-8263-8
        EBook   978-1-9845-8262-1

Print information available on the last page

Rev. date: 07/09/2020

TOMMY
Takes Back His
POWER

RICHARD WHITE

Tommy was dreaming that he hit Billy the Bully and he fell harder than a giant that stood ten feet tall, although Tommy only stood five feet even and was eleven years old. When Tommy hit Billy, Billy hit the ground. Dirt flew up in the air long with his school books. The neighborhood boys stood near the wall where the fight started, giving one another high fives and laughing because Billy the Bully just got punched. While the others just smiled to them selves saying that they were happy somebody had finally got that little punk. The school kids were jumping up and down and cheering so loudly of what they were witnessing.

Billy and his two-man crew always did mean things to the children in the neighborhood after Tommy acted as if he was going to hit Billy's crew with his fist, which caused them to take off running. He left Billy the Bully on the ground seeing stars. Tommy had seen enough bullying from them. Billy would always snatch his lunch money or hit his book out of his hands. Tommy felt like a hero that day for once in his life.

Tommy! Tommy! Tommy, it is time to wake up for school. You are going to be late again and I do not have time to take you this morning or I will be late and I cannot afford to miss any time from work. No sir, not today," Tommy's mother said, And I love you.

Good morning! I hope your morning is going well, "Tommy mumbled as he kicked the covers off his body and got out of bed. He looked in the mirror and begun to mimic his mother last words, I do not have time to take you to school this morning, as he walks to the bathroom to brush his teeth. He took his precious time because Tommy wanted to miss the bus again because Billy the Bully and his crew had been bullying him again making fun of his clothes, taking his snack money, and calling him mean names. When Billy and his crew are around everyone is unhappy. Billy and his crew were best known for throwing balled-up paper at their peers and beating them up daily. When the students went home from school, they hid from their parents and cried in their rooms. The only days the kids felt relief was on the weekends.

Tommy! Tommy! Tommy! His mother called out. Yes, yes Tommy replied. Breakfast is ready. Come on before you miss the bus, his mother said. Coming now, Tommy replied as he rushed down the step. The smell of sausage and eggs hit his nose. Tommy rubbed his belly. His mother handed him some sausage and eggs then kissed him. Have a wonderful day, Tommy mother said. She noticed some hesitation in his movement and him not wanting to leave the house. She asked is everything was okay. Yeah, Mom he replied. Tommy did not want to tell her about the bullying, and he did not want to go to school, so he proceeded out of the house.

Outside, Tommy saw Billy the Bully, but Billy did not see him. Billy and his crew were beating up a cat. Billy was punching the cat while his crew was holding the cat. One of Billy crew members noticed Tommy coming out of his house and stopped Billy from hitting the cat and pointed at Tommy eating his food. Billy hid behind a parked car.

"Hey, Ms. Susan, how is your day going? Tommy asked Ms. Susan who was out watering her flowerbed. She loved to water her flowerbed and lawn early in the morning to beat the sun. I am doing fine and yourself? Was her response. I'm doing fine too." Tommy said.

I haven't been seeing you lately she said. My mother has been bringing me to school because I have been waking up late. Tommy said. After speaking to Ms. Susan, Tommy continue to walk to the bus stop. He was looking high and low for Billy and his crew. Not seeing them, he let out a deep breath thinking that he was in the clear….until he felt a punch to his face, causing him to drop his food.

As Billy was cocking back, getting ready to hit him again, Tommy took off running toward the bus stop with Billy and his crew right on his tail. Tommy ran so fat that it kicked dust in the air causing Billy to wipe his eyes. As Tommy made it to the bus stop the bus was just pulling up. He was saved by the bus because the bus driver did not tolerate any nonsense or bullying.

Everything was going well in school until math class came. Tommy and Billy were in the same math class. As soon as Mr. White finished giving his morning speech and turned around to start writing on the chalkboard, the paper throwing started. Tommy shook his head mumbling to himself he will get Billy one day. Then his mother's words came into his thoughts. Be a person of character no matter what. So, Tommy shook the thought about beating up Billy the bully and his crew. He just sat there trying to figure out another way so he can get the bullying to stop. No ideas came to mind, so he just focused on Mr. White teaching the class.

Eleven o'clock came it was lunchtime. The bell rang, and the school hallways were filled with kids rushing to the lunchroom to get Ms. Smith's special lemon pepper wings and fries, and strawberry juice. All the kids went crazy over those wings on Friday's. Tommy ran through the hallways superfast. He wanted to be the first one in the lunchroom. He knew Billy would take his food if he didn't hurry up and eat. Tommy was so hungry because Billy caused him to drop his breakfast. As soon as he received his lunch tray, Billy came from out of no where tapping him on his shoulder. Tommy shoved his tray toward Billy's direction. He did not get a chance to eat any wings or fries. Attention! Attention! Attention! Students of St. Rosy. All students who have lunch detention, report to room 206 as soon as you get your lunch tray and that includes Billy Woods, the school principal said on the intercom. The lunchroom went in an uproar because everyone knew that they were going to eat their lunch with no worries today. Billy grabbed two of Tommy chicken wings before leaving to serve his lunch detention. The second bell was ringing ending lunch. Tommy arrived at history class in the nick of time.

Mrs. Jones informed the class on what she will be teaching on in history like she normally does. Mrs. Jones added always be a leader not a follower be fair to each other. Do not mind skin color. We are all one. The school bell rang, and the school day is over. On the bus ride home, Tommy gave what Mrs. Jones said some serious thought about becoming a leader and being a voice for the kids like himself that were being pushed and shoved around.

Upon looking up, Tommy saw Billy in the front of the bus, and he already knew he was up to no good. Normally, Billy would sit at the back of the bus so him sitting in front only meant two things: either the driver told him to sit there because he knew what Billy was doing to the other kids or Billy was up to something. Whatever the case, Tommy hoped that he could make it home in one piece to his loving mother. As the bus arrived at the bus stop, Tommy thought to himself man the ride home seem shorter. Did the bus take a shortcut?

Billy and his boys rushed off the bus as if they had something important to do. All the kids felt relieved because for the first time in a while they could walk home with no fear. They were all disappointed when they saw Billy hiding behind a parked truck waiting to attack. Everyone hoped that it would not be them. Tommy thought that they were gone because he was second to last getting off the bus, and he did not see him in front of him. So, when Tommy walked past the front of the truck. Billy tripped Tommy from behind causing him to hit the pavement face first. When Tommy hit the ground, he did not know if he should just lay still or jump up and take off running. Before he could do either Billy grabbed him by the ankles turned him upside down causing everything that was in his pockets to come out on the ground. Tommy tried to put himself in a balled-up position, but it did not work. Billy got tired of holding Tommy and dropped Tommy to the ground, and Tommy took off running. Billy chased Tommy. As Tommy was running, he nearly got hit by a car that was passing by in the street. The driver hit the brakes as soon as he noticed them running. But Billy wasn't so lucky. Billy was hit by the car causing him to injure his leg. He cried out in pain.

A crowd started to run toward where Billy laid on the ground crying. Tommy was confused about whether he should help Billy or go home. Tommy decided to go back and help. His mother's word came into thought about being a person of good character and integrity. An ambulance was called, and Billy was taken to the hospital. Billy foot was broken. He received a cast on his leg and was released from the hospital that night.

Tommy dusted off his clothes upon making it through his front door. He knew his mother would fuss if she saw how dirty his clothes were. As Tommy entered the house, he smelled his mother's famous roast with gravy, steamed rice, and peas. When she heard the front door open Tommy's mother called out his name. Yes, mom he replied. Nothing. Just checking to make sure that was you, baby she said. The second he made it to the kitchen his mother stopped what she was doing so she could give him a kiss and a hug. In the mist of giving Tommy a kiss and a hug his mother noticed his swollen face and torn clothes.

What happened? Was his mother's anxious question as she rushed over to Tommy. Tommy informed her about what have been going on the whole school year about Billy the bully been bullying him, Billy getting hit by a car, and the accident broke one of Billy's leg. He also told his mom he remained a person of good character and he went back to help Billy. Tommy mother hugged him as tightly as she could. She wanted him to feel he was loved and how proud she was of him. Tommy mothers informed him that he did the right thing by going back to help Billy, but she was also disappointed that he did not tell her he was being bullied for over a year. Tommy informed his mother about starting a bullying foundation.

Stevie Rae is a student Billy bulled. She is an honor student that never bothered anyone, and Billy picked on Stevie Rae for years. He would do things to her like pull her hair, throw food at her, eat whatever he wanted off her school lunch tray, and Billy pushed her and knocked her to the floor a few times.

Stevie Rae had enough of Billy's bullying. One day, she sat in her bedroom and wrote a letter to her parents explaining what she had been going through at school. She wrote that Billy, Sean, and Will had been mentally and physically harassing her and she had enough. Stevie Rae committed suicide. When they got to her room, they were shocked by what they saw. Her father ran and grabbed her. Her mother cried out in horror and ran to call 911. When she got back to the room she noticed the note on her bed. Before she could even read one word, she fell to her knees besides her daughter in disbelief and pain.

Tommy's mom said the she would help him every step of the way. The next day, Tommy reached out to Stevie Rae's parents and told them that he was starting an anti-bullying foundation in honor of Stevie Rae. The following Saturday, they all stood on street corner with signs that read, "stop bullying!" the whole neighborhood showed up and gave support. Tommy and his mother just looked at each other and smiled. They knew that they were doing the right thing. Even after being hit by the car, Billy showed up to support the cause. Billy had decided to change his ways.

After the anti-bullying rally, Billy and Tommy became great friends. Tommy and Billy begun to hang out regularly. At times, Billy would invite Tommy over to his house to watch sports like football, basketball, and soccer. Tommy enjoyed every minute of it, especially since he didn't have a lot of guy friends. Also, because Tommy's father had passed away when he was incredibly young. Tommy was too young to remember his father or his funeral, but he always remembered yearning for a father figure, especially when he saw other kids with their father playing around. So, hanging out at Billy's house always made him feel like he was cool, and life was good. Stevie Rae's parents decided to have a dinner in honor of Stevie Rae. They invited everyone that was involved in getting the anti bullying foundation started. They even invited Billy. He was nervous because he knew that his old crew and himself were responsible for Stevie Rae passing. The dinner was held at the school gym because of the large crowd.

At the anti-bullying rally, Tommy along with Stevie Rae's parents and his mother gave a speech on how the anti-bullying foundation was created.

Hi! Hello to everyone. I would like to give thanks to you all. My name is Tommy and I have been being bullied for the last five years of my life. I am tired of being bullied and seeing my friends bullied as well. I used to be scared to go to school because of bullying. I was ashamed to tell anyone because I did not want them to think I was lame or a snitch, so I did not tell anyone. Many nights, I felt hopeless. Tommy could not get another word out of his mouth; tears formed in his eyes.

He cleared his throat and continued. Bullying caused a dear friend of mine to end her life. Stevie Rae was not just a classmate: she was someone special. I believe if she had some one to talk to things would have turned out different. This foundation is in honor of her. Tommy put his right hand in a balled fist and yells from the top of his lungs, no more bullying! No more bullying! Everyone in the gym stood up and started saying, "no more bullying! No more bullying! Then Billy the bully made his way on stage. As he was making it on stage the people who didn't see him apologized to Stevie Rae parents and Tommy's family had a confused look and others booed him.

Once Billy was fully on stage, he paused for a second to apologize once more to everyone. Once Billy started speaking loud laughter could be heard causing Billy to stop speaking and to see where it was coming from. Sean and Will were yelling at the top of their lungs. Billy you are a sellout! We are supposed to bully people forever. We don't want to be your friend anymore. You are a sucker like the rest of these people. Sean and Will were asked to leave.

At that moment, Billy was questioning himself about the choice that he made to join Tommy's foundation. Those words that Sean and Will yelled made him feel under pressure. Billy knew that strategy all too well because he taught it to them.

Being under pressure was something Billy wasn't used to. Tommy stepped in for Billy. Don't let them words affect this beautiful moment. This moment is in honor of Stevie Rae. Tommy informed Billy. Billy managed to shake Sean and Will words. As Billy was stepping up to the mic. He glanced back toward Stevie Rae's parents and seeing them smile gave Billy the confidence that he was lacking at the moment. Billy started speaking hello to everyone some of you may know my name. my name is Billy and to those who do not know my name is Billy the ex-bully. I said ex- bully because I was that until I broke my leg. Me and those guys that were escorted out used to bully our peers. I apologize for my actions and behalf of those guys that were asked to leave. I just learned from Tommy and Stevie Rae's parents that my myself and my crew were the cause of Stevie Rae's passing. I would like to apologize to everyone in the room whom I might have hurt mentally and physically. I thought being a bully was the coolest thing in the world. I was truly misguided. I was copying my older brother's and his friends' which were wrong. I really did not know that people were being affected even at their homes.

The crowd said "Aww." Billy continued. When I got hit by the car, "My life flashed before my eyes, and I could not get up off the ground. I was hurting and cried for help. My so-called friends just stood on the corner giving each other high fives and laughing at me. That's not a friend. Friends always have your back whether you are up or down. On the day of the accident, I was chasing Tommy, and Tommy came back and give me a hand. He didn't care about the looks he received from his friends. Seeing all the pain and hurt that I caused, I know that I needed to work with this foundation so we can stop bullying.

And that was Billy's speech. The entire crowd applauded him, while others waited until he came off the stage and shook his hand. Stevie Rae's parents announced that they will be an honor dinner at Tre's Diner. As Billy was leaving the event, Sean and Will were waiting off to the side, away from everyone. "Yo, Billy! Over here," Sean called out while using his hands signaling him to come. "What's up, fellas"? What you all doing hanging out here? This isn't you all thing, Billy said. You are right. This isn't our type of thing, but we are here to see what's gotten into you." Will replied with an attitude. The accident changed me. I am different, Billy said. "We the bully gang for life," Sean said as he hit his chest with a balled fist.

Before Billy could respond to Sean's statement Tommy came looking for Billy. Billy! Billy! Billy! Tommy yelled, "Here I am," Billy yelled back. Tommy made his way over to where Will, Sean, and Billy were standing. Tommy noticed Sean's and Will's attitude were not friendly, so he told Billy he was just checking to see if he was still coming to the honor dinner. Yeah, I am still rolling Billy answered in cool manner. Billy informed his old crew that he needs to go. Then he followed Tommy.

Tre's Diner was packed to its capacity. A picture of Stevie Rae was hanging in the restaurant. Stevie Rae's parents gave a speech about how they appreciated everyone for coming out to give support in honor of their daughter. They even mentioned that they knew Stevie Rae was looking down from heaven and thanking everyone as well. Everyone gave Billy a round of applause for his bravery. Everyone enjoyed the dinner. As everyone was exiting the restaurant, Sean and Will went to Billy putting his arms around him as if they were his crutches. Tommy saw this and quickly approached them from behind and startled Billy, Sean and Will. "Are you all right, Billy?" Tommy asked. "Yes, I'm fine, just talking to Sean and Will. Billy assured him. Tommy said. Sean jumped in and said, "We'll get him home. My daddy will be here in a few minutes. I called him on my cellphone already." Tommy looked at Billy who shook his head and walked off. Billy yelled, "I'll be okay, I promise."

Printed in the United States
By Bookmasters